The RED BARN

Nat Baldwin

The Red Barn.

ISBN: 978-1-940853-10-9

Designed and published by Calamari Archive, Ink.

www.calamariarchive.com

For Amanda.

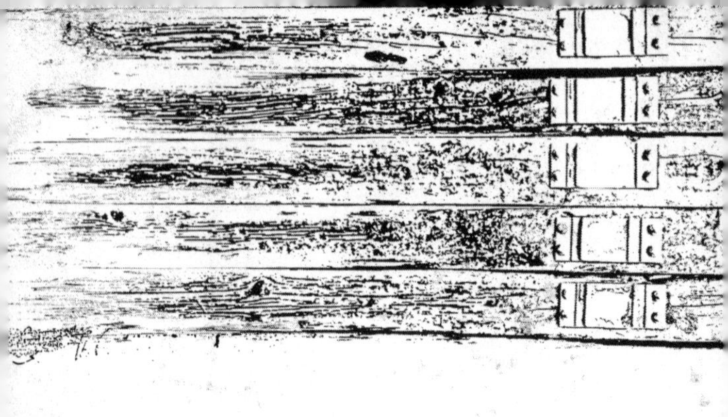

Thanks go to the editors of the following publications where these stories first appeared: *crag*, *PANK*, *Alice Blue*, *The Spectacle*, *Fanzine*, *MCFX--An Anthology of the First 10 Years of the Mission Creek Festival*, *Deluge*, *Timber*, *Sleepingfish* and *DIAGRAM*.

Special thanks to Peter Markus and Derek White for helping shape these words into a book. Additional thanks to Joyelle McSweeney, Noy Holland, and Blake Butler. Thanks to my mother and my father and my brother.

I.

II.

III.

The RED BARN
6

I.
7

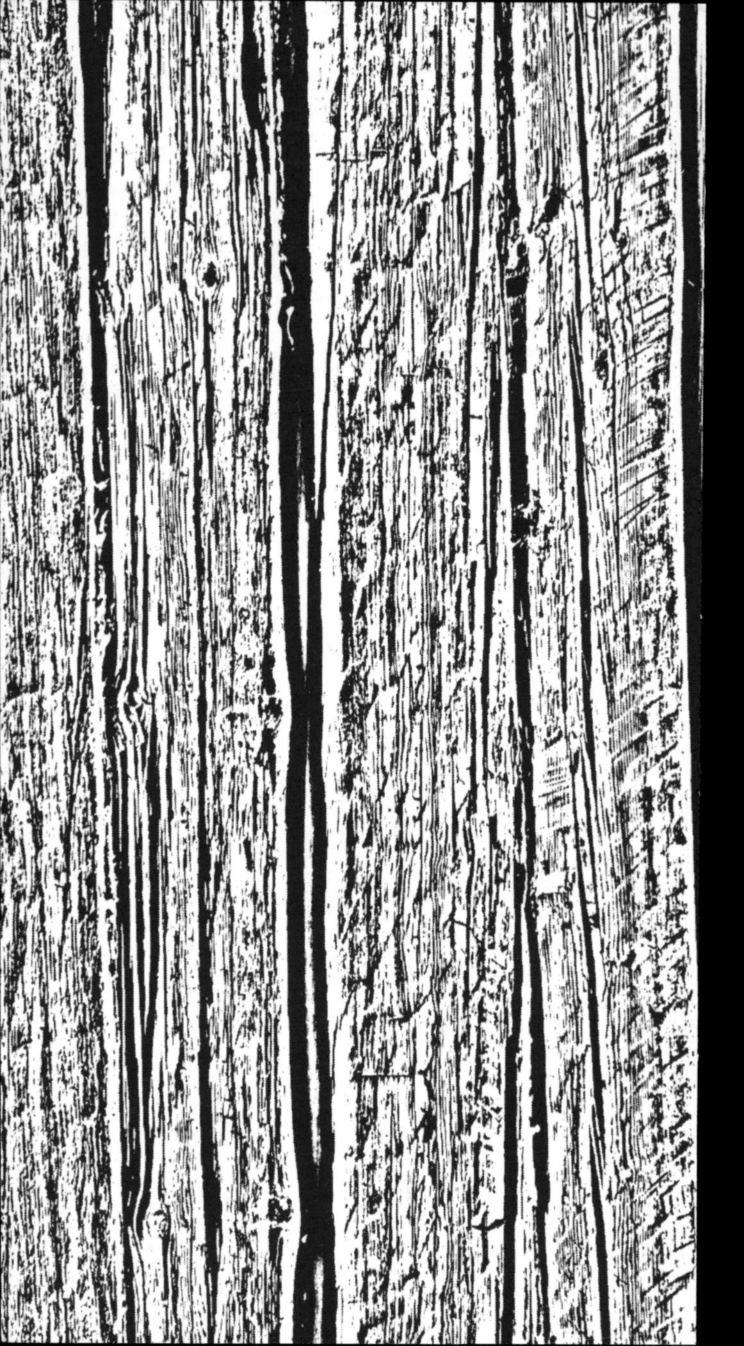

A Crack in the Back of the Barn

I watch through a crack in the back of the barn. The sound tears up from the gut through the throat. They say it is the stress before the sound that taints the quality of meat. The blade sticks beneath fatty pockets of the face. When handle meets skin the body gets stuck. The cut runs down the throat to the chest. The knife must not twist. They hold the weight down to drain the blood out. If they step too close to the kicks a leg bone can break. I have seen a shin split clean in two. They cut the tendons running through the center of the hooves. These they fasten with a chain and hook. They drag it then to the barrel where scalding water waits. The water must not reach a boil. They hoist the body up. Rising steam meets the carcass where it hangs. The body, in the sun, all muscle and meat.

The men lower the carcass in the barrel. I watch from the barn's roof. They let the meat soak till the skin burns off. When the skin has scorched off they turn the body over.

The men wear hats on their heads, straps hanging loose from their belts. I can see teeth in their mouths, the dirt on their hands. The barn is not far from the shed, the creek, the woods.

They unhook the chain and clamp the hook in the mouth.

Sunlight glints off wires and metal, the eye of the hook.

From the top of the barn I can see the house through the trees. I used to watch the lights flicker on and off at night. Now the windows are boarded up with wood, the leaves on the branches dead.

In the dirt around the barrel: crates, buckets, wires, hoses, hammers, pipes, barrows, shovels, boots, trucks, rakes, tires, balers, axes, engines, grinders, cutters, scythes, sickles, mowers, shanks, tractors, chisels, plows, puddles, shit, mud, glass, ashes, tubs.

They use the blades to scrape.

The blades must be hot to scald the skin off or to peel. There can be no hair left on the skin to scrape. Nothing on the nipples or toes. They pour water from a bucket, rub the skin with the bell of a scraper. They scoop hay beneath the belly with a shovel. Wash the blood and bile, pluck black nails loose with a hook. Hose down the dirt and the skin and the soot. The meat must not soil. The meat must not spoil.

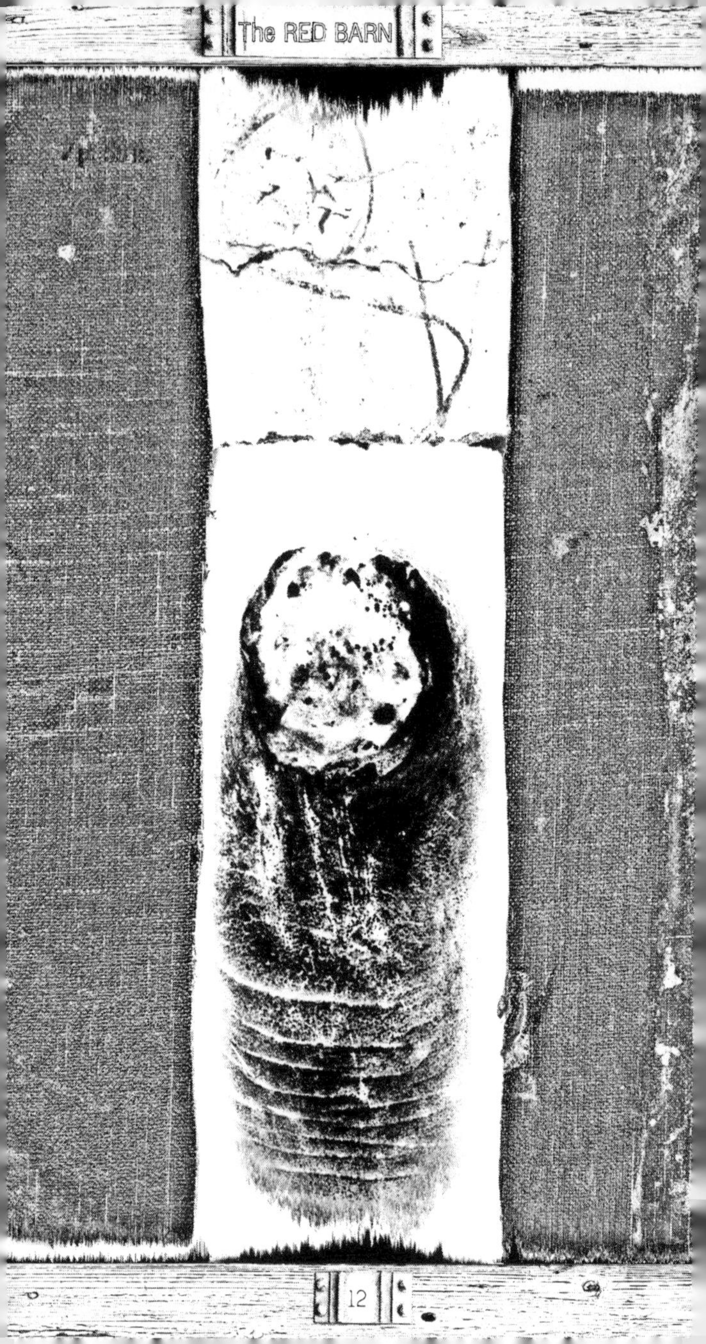

Rabbits out Back in the Burn Pile

When we first met he said it was on account of an accident with a car. His skin, puffed out, swollen, ashen and bruised. He could barely make words from his mouth. There were cuts on his face and hands, drool on his chin. He pointed to speak. A nail his finger did not possess. The spot where the nail used to be was wet, a color lighter than the rest of his finger.

There was a plastic container with a long spout in his lap. He sat in his chair and said nothing, eyes closed. He opened his mouth, pressed it hard against the container. His neck loosened, the container dropped to the dirt. Liquid spilled from its spout.

We wheeled him from one place to the next, or dragged his body by hand. He would lie in the grass out back, or on the burnt mattress in the frontyard. Or on the rocks by the brook. If we found him we dragged him back up the hill, into the house. Our faces would burn if we did not do this. Sometimes, even if we dragged him back to where he belonged, we would still get punished.

I answered the ad in the paper.

I arrived ready to tend animals, sow crops, plow fields, slash weeds, clean pens, butcher meat, milk cattle, fix the barn.

There were no animals, no crops.

My room was in the basement. I was alone when I got there.

I was not alone in the basement when I woke up.

The one that posted the ad in the paper said it was just rabbits out back in the burn pile. There were rabbits in the yard, I remember, but the bone they found was too big to be rabbit. There was flesh still attached to bone. I did not see it but that is what they said.

The one that posted the ad said the rabbits were cremated. When they found sneakers the story changed. They found little else in the basement.

Other things found in the burn pile: knife handle, melted blade, tree limb clippers, chair.

One day I found his body along the shore. All around him, sticking in and out of the rocks, were branches, scattered, broken. I heard no storm in the night while I slept. I could see the back of his head, hair, top of scalp. His skin stretched tight against his bones, cracked and seared. The back of his body had scars raised from the skin, running from just below the shoulder blade, down through the backbone, to the other side of the ribs. I could not see legs, just rocks where legs should be. He said nothing when I said his name.

They said the hay was still burning when they got there. Pruning shears stuck out of a barrel. The one that posted the ad was covered in ash and soot.

They dumped the barrel out on a blue tarp and sifted through the pile. They found bones, teeth. The bones, off-white, brittle, not yet charred. The teeth still sharp.

The one that posted the ad said he split his head on the tub.

She did not want a body like that to be seen they said.

She did not say his name, called him something else.

She unbuttoned her black shirt below her breasts.

There were pieces of wood broken on the rocks around his body. The wood had nails sticking out. If the nails were dull or sharp I could not tell. I scraped them on a rock. Tapped them with my fist. With rust I wrote on the rocks. Traced the lines of bones in my hands. Not all the nails were rusty. I ripped the old nails out and piled them on the rocks. Picked up a piece of wood and moved his head into the light. Where his eyes looked there was no way to tell.

The gate was closed but not locked. The fence did not look like the fence. Barbed wire coiled along the top. No burnt mattress in the frontyard. The grass had grown so high where the mattress once was I could not see it from the gate.

The house had words written across the siding. The words bled into each other. The windows were battened with wood, the wood nailed into the siding. If people still lived in the house they would not see out.

The basement did not have windows to see out. It did not have beds or blankets, so when we slept we slept on dirt.

He did not stay in the basement. When he did not sleep on the burnt mattress in the frontyard he slept in the bathtub in the house. We were not allowed inside the room with the tub. We were told if we tried to go in that room we would not come out.

Below the eyes a half moon of flesh raised. The skin looked hard, as if a rock got lodged beneath. The nose, flat. The skin of the nose was not split. The bone of the nose pointed down to the mouth. Shadow shaded the upper lip. Lines on each side of the mouth turned up and in toward the nose. The mouth, pulled taut toward the cheeks, was shut. The lower lip, full. Below it were the same burns that marked the eyebrows, the upper lip. The rest of the skin was smooth. The bone of the chin curved up to the ears, the lobes shapeless and pale. Hair hung down past the cheeks but did not reach as far as the neck. The neck sunk into the rocks and sticks. I grabbed a fistful of hair.

I walked up the front steps and turned the knob on the front door of the house. The door was locked. I picked up a rock and threw it through the door and once opened stepped inside. Down into the basement I went. There was glass in the dirt I cut my foot on. I walked up to the room with the bathtub. Put my foot under the faucet. No water came out. The tub was black. A layer of dust had settled on top of the blackness. Nails stuck out of the window sill. I ripped one from the wood, wet it with my tongue. Scraped the black of the tub with the tip of the nail. Wiped the black specks down the drain with my hands and feet. Then I laid down in the tub. Scratched at my skin with the nail until the tip went dull. I bit the nail between my teeth and swallowed rust. I ripped the rest of the nails from the wood. Filled the tub to the top.

From a hook in the barn a harness hung. I slung it on my back and returned to the rocks. I started with the collar, the crown of the head. Wrapped the throat-latch tight. The buckle stuck in neck skin. The slack I loosened. The breast strap looped more than once around the chest. I tied the hip strap between the legs, roped the reins round my waist. Gave a quick tug and metal dug into the cheeks. The lips pulled back, baring teeth. I gripped the pole with both hands, dragged the body through the rocks up the hill to the barn. It was too damp in the barn to leave the body on the floor. I lifted it by the chain and left it from the hook hanging. Light hit the face through holes in the roof.

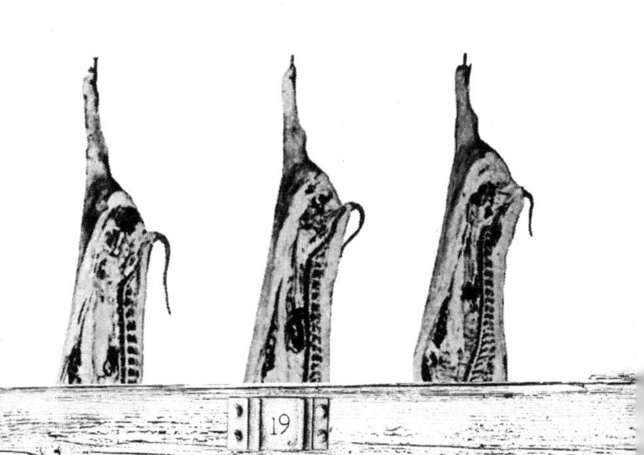

The RED BARN
20

The Stalls in the Barn

Into bales or bundles I gather hay. Sometimes I stack it loose with a pitchfork. The tines must not be dull or rusted. Cut hay needs to cure properly or it becomes coarse. I must not be too quick with the rake, must not wait too long. The rows must be straight. If there is too much moisture in the hay it rots. If rotten hay is eaten it can cause infection. A hole burns through the lining of a stomach. Moist hay is also at risk to combust. When steam rises off the hay I shove a crowbar in the stack and twist. I rise at dawn to muck the stalls in the barn. Shovel floors and scrape walls and brush bodies. Remove bedding, soiled and wet. Dump dirty water buckets out in the bushes. Scrub clumps and bits of hay from buckets. When I cannot find a brush I use a handful of hay. I fill the buckets back up, the troughs full of grains. Check along the walls for loose nails sticking out. In the dark stalls it is difficult to see. I tighten bolts and screws and hinges on doors. Loop ropes in knots around poles at night. They sleep standing up or on their sides or stomachs.

They snore and twitch.

They do not sleep much.

The Red Barn

I.

With my fist I scrape the taste out. Drop my pack to the dirt. The kids huddle close in the dark. We will soon get to work. But now no one can talk. I lock the latch. Take out the new tools. Tell the kids that today we will work all day. Point to the door bolted shut. They turn in unison, nod their heads yes. I point to windows, boarded up and black. I say how will we know when today's day is done? Their blank faces stare. When we are done with the work is how we will know, I say. It may be a long day. Or maybe many days. But first things first. We need to clean the new tools thick with dust from the town. I say to the kids form a straight line. They hold their little hands out. Open their empty mouths. Take in their hands the tools I hand them. Lick the dust from the tools with the wet of their tongues. Then they pass the tools back to my hand. I examine their work. Most miss spots. Only one passes. The good kid again. So I set him aside. Hand him a new tool. I advise him to aim for the backs of their heads. I whisper in his ear so no one else can hear. I say just one strike, that much work lies ahead. But do not take it easy on them. When the good kid is done I lead him into the shed. Wipe him down. Adjust all his angles. Strip the clothes from his skin. He knows to keep quiet. I say you have done good. More words I whisper. He closes his eyes. The good kid listens.

2.

He calls the mud dust. We call him Father. He wipes the mud stuck to his skin. We wipe it up off the floor. The floor caked with dirt. The mud turns to dirt when it dries. Our skin dries out in the dark. The barn in darkness all day. We do not know our names. Or where we lived before. Or how we came to be. But we cannot ask. He slaps us in the face. Knees us in the teeth. Our mouths fill up with blood. The blood drips from our lips. He smears it back into our mouths. Makes us choke it down. Makes us say his name. He calls our new names numbers. But they always seem to change. Or we do not recall their shape. Or just mishear the pitch. Today we clean the tools. New tools slicked thick with mud. He dragged them back from town. The town we have never seen. One day one of us tried to escape. He did not make it far. Now he hangs by a beam above. We nailed right through his hands. In the morning I open my eyes. He is the first sight I see. Body calm and still. Light drained from skin. Darker shades each day. I rise when Father calls.

3.

We stand still in a circle. In the center of our circle stands an animal. Its fur darkened in spots. It is unclear if the spots are natural markings, or tracks of blood and mud. The animal bleeds from its throat. We are lucky to be locked in the barn. The woods not safe for kids. My parents were not parents to me. They left me there alone. Father told me everything. I remember nothing. That is all I need to know. When Father enters the barn, the animal in the center collapses to the dirt. The animal spreads away from itself, shapeless but for its unblinking eyes. We freeze. Father barks orders. We follow his words. Grab the tools. Sweep the animal up. Some of us do not work fast enough. When we slow or slack we get slapped in the back with a branch. Father knows what we need. The last crack hits me hard in the center of the spine. I will work harder next time are the words in my mind as I fall face first. I am not certain if the feeling of splitting is in my skin or bones or both. A sharp light flickers through my eyes as they close. The last thing I see atop the remains piled neat in the dirt are the two bulging eyes of the animal. I do not feel the impact of ground.

4.

He leaves every night right in the middle of it when we are some of us sleeping but others tossing and shifting in our beds spiked with feather and bone and scraps of fur found from animals that died or not yet living ripped from their skins or insides of their guts and dried on the lines that hang from the beams next to the boy to remind us that we are not to escape and we will not survive and that the world does not want us in its outside light and that this is our world here in this barn where we belong and he taught us this so that is how we know and there is no one else to believe but the man who saved us from our slight lives and how do we know if we deserve it or not and who else to owe though I cannot recall how we got found or where we were before the barn door shut and was it worse back there back then and we just buried it down deep or washed it out clean and have now come to believe this is the place where we need to begin and this is the man we need to lead us so I lie here and wonder where he goes as he does each night and what will I do if he does not return and I cannot find sleep or stop all the shaking but then the sound of steps up the hill and the door creaking and before the hot feeling of skin soft and sinking I exhale a deep breath and thank god and dream blank and thank god.

5.

I still do not know what he was reaching for. None of us do. This was before he tried to escape. Before we had to hammer nails through his hands. The boy had been acting strange for some time. His mind seemed shot. Color drained from his eyes. He was often sent to the shed. In odd intervals he spoke. The sounds his mouth made muddled into drone, or took large tonal leaps, discomfiting and dissonant, with quick shifts in volume to match. He always fell from his trance into catatonic silence. Never have I seen such vacancy in a face, a body. I stumbled upon him many days thinking he was dead, kicked him in his ribs and head till he twitched. Maybe that is what he wanted when he reached into the flames. He grabbed a handful he could not hold, left his arm there hanging. His skin smoked and popped like liquid hitting a hot pan. He bubbled up and blackened. A rotten smell filled the barn. His eyes widened but still looked empty. His mouth loosened up but no sound came out. We did not know how to react so we did not.

6.

A bright blood trail drips from a dog's mouth. A mouth filled with feathers stuck to the body of a bird. The bird's body enmeshed in the dog's jagged teeth. I see hot smoky breath puff through the gaps. A haze swells around the dog's head and the bleeding dead bird. But the dog bleeds too, thru a gash on its neck. It does not spill out as with the bird but just shines wet and still. Looks sticky. The dog starts to circle, does not know where to go. He tracks blood across more and more of our floor. The dog drools. The dirt darkens, clots to the consistency of mud. The bird's shape deflates. In the dog's mouth the emptying space fills with froth. Thick spit mixes its white with the red blood of the dead bird. The colors do not blend. They swirl and snake up against and all around each other never quite congealing. The dog's wide spasmodic circles turn tight and focused, spinning itself in place. The blood does not drip so much now as spray. I do not take my eyes off the dog or bird or the arc of blood.

7.

Skin goes numb, limbs act without thought. I get stopped by a wall, a fist, a fire, a branch. My jaw unhinges, slacks toward my throat. Drool pools off my chin. Sound fizzles out. I wake up blacked out. They circle me. Tie up my hands and feet. They drag me in dirt. The dirt soaks me up. Dogs lick most of my skin. They lather parts made thick by dirt. Everything becomes mud. Their teeth feel hot. Birds peck my cheeks. I hold still. Hold on to the heat. A feeling I can name. I see hands holding tools. Eyes unblinking. The sound of teeth gnawing. A slow grinding of meat. Then no heat left. The ground below blurs. I rise slow to the roof. My hands spread out. Arms outstretch.

Head droops loose. I see a nail in my hand. The nail disappears. It takes more than one strike. Shoots through the other side. All my feeling rushes back.

8.

I uncoil rope from my pack. The rope unused and stiff. I spool it out straight on the dirt. The kids line up in a row. Taking care to step clear of the rope. Their weight will weaken it. One time a rope split in half on a back. Sometimes they do not listen. They stepped on the strands leaving dead spots in the core. I leave nails spiked from the floor. Leave the old rope tied to a beam. It is still soaked with blood from the back. I can not recall which kid took the hit. They all carve the same shape in my eyes over time. I have since used a branch. But some branches break in my hand on impact. Some land the wrong way on a bone. A rope gets even returns. I grab the new one laying at their feet. Get a feel for its weight. Run my fingers over the braids. Rub my face along the bristles. I start between shins and ankles. They know to not look down. Or make any sound with their mouths. When I am done I stand to my feet. Stare into the blanks of their eyes. I tell them take a step. The lock on the door I unlatch.

9.

We stare away from the light down at the dirt and listen to the pulse of his voice and all of its counting while we dig dirt loose and place the loosened dirt in fresh new piles just to push it back later back into the hole hollowed out by our hands and the tools they grip without the good sense of what could lie below or if there is any breath left but there is no way to know and no we will not ask 'cause we know he knows and that he knows best and yes we know that and skin burns as it splits the sun beats at our backs dripping puddles at our feet soaking into the mud and the caking at our ankles from openings in shins blending in to the dogs crying out from their throats and sticking on teeth that dull life into death while we pray without words for new ways to be found and we smooth out the last patch of dirt with our mouths.

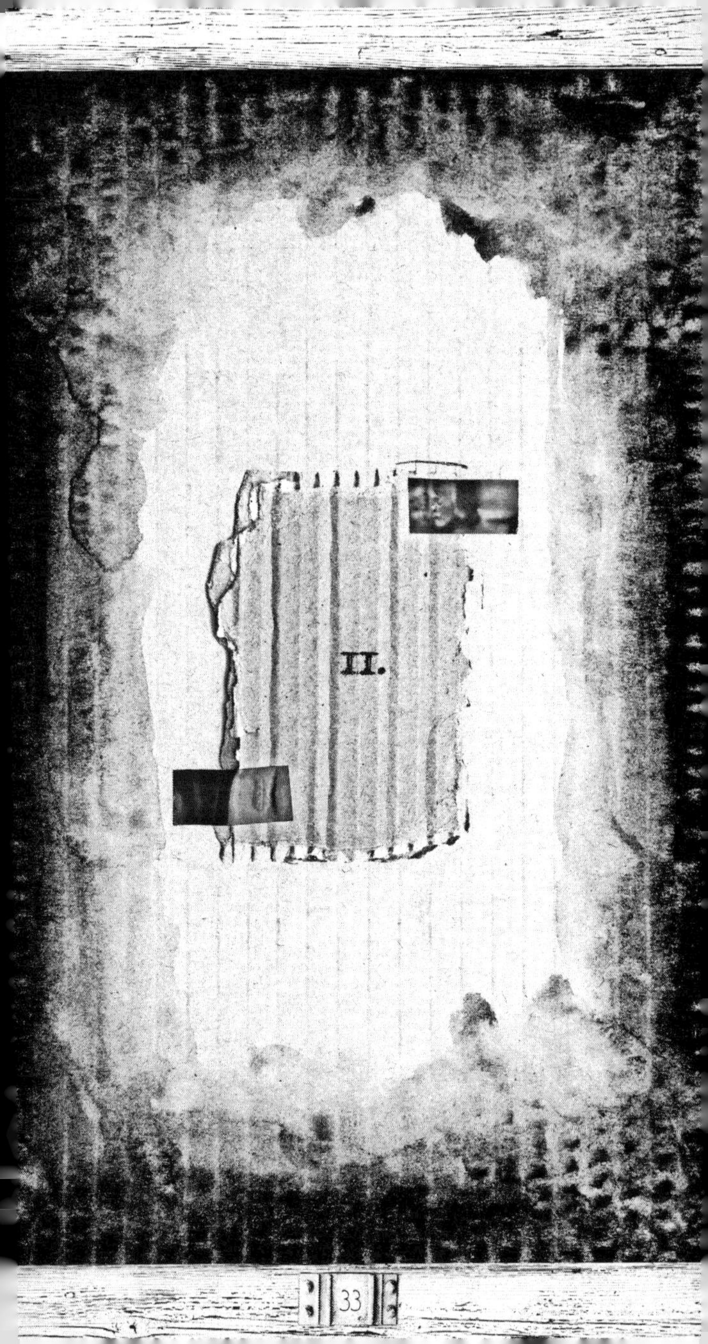
II.

The Shape of a Face

The father is down in the street. The porch light flickers. I sip liquid from a glass. Stare up at branches or into the light. See the father twitch. I look straight at the father as light hits him head-on. No scratches on his face. The street is not close. I lift the glass to my lips. Kill the porch light and take a step toward the father. See the skin on his chest. There is less light in the street. I trip on a rake in the grass. The father sits up. His face blurs. I tip the glass back and make my way back up the steps. Flip the porch light back on and refill my glass. The porch light is weak. A branch breaks from a tree. The father sits still. The outline of a chest. The shape of a face. No other sound. I touch the glass to my mouth and it becomes light. I rub the light on my face.

I feel nothing. Another branch falls not far from the father. The father is still. I let the glass go.

The Father's Face

The brother knows I do not like dirt on my skin. When there is dirt on my skin I always try to peel it. When I peel the dirt with my nails the dirt turns to mud. I wipe the mud with my palm and lick it. I would rather have mud taste in my mouth than dirt caked and cracking on my skin.

The light blinds, the chain loosens. The brother drops to the floor. The weight of him shakes the wood. I lift my face from the voice.

The sound does not sound like the sound of brother.

I do not know the word. He keeps saying father, father, keeps saying corpse. I do not know what it is but I like the sound. He kicks my mouth with his boots.

I spit out a tooth. Nails poke through the wood of the floor. We stop at the glass in front of the chair where sits a man. No skin on his face. Mouth open. No sound in his mouth.

The brother lifts the chain, high above his head, says the word father.

Then he says the word not father.

He says the word again and again and again and again and again and again and again.

The father's face rots, blackened to bone.

The brother walks back from the kitchen, hammer in hand.

Says the word maggot.

I look at black holes the father's eyes once filled.

The brother puts the claw in his mouth. I hear the scrape of teeth against steel. He picks a piece out with a nail. Lifts his finger to my mouth and wipes it on my lips.

He looks me in the face.

He says hold still.

The chain falls from my neck.

My skin in the teeth of the chain.

On the floor I crawl. I cannot see the brother. The chair empty, I drag my body to it. Call out to the brother. Hear a tap on the glass. Nothing but dirt. The father crawls out of it. Father's body not a corpse. Cannot see his face. In his hand, the hand of the brother. He drags brother to the ditch. The ditch at the end of the road that runs into the river. I watch them disappear into the ditch. I wait and watch. When the bodies rise up mud covers the brother. He runs ahead of the father. The father walks slow. Holds up a shovel. I lose sight of the brother. Forget to watch brother watching the father. The father walks up to the glass, presses his face to it. Bugs, maggots, no eyeballs in sockets. All that is intact on his face are teeth. His teeth tap at the glass. I am in the chair. The father lifts his arm above his head. Holds the brother by the hair. The face of the brother muddy. The father walks backwards and does not drop the brother. He does not stop looking through the glass. He lets go of the brother. Flips him around face down in the dirt. Smears his face in it. Lifts the shovel up, brings the shovel down. Cracks the brother's skull. In the dirt digs a hole. The hole bigger than the body of the brother. He drops the brother in the dirt.

Does not drop the brother in the hole. The father steps to the hole's edge. Looks down, then up to the sky. Lets his body fall. Clouds of dirt rise up from the hole. The brother lifts his head. Wipes mud from his eyes. He pushes dirt back down into the hole. I watch brother watch the father's face fill with dirt.

When the hole fills to the top the brother lies on his back. Mud spills from the sides of his mouth.

The brother says the father is not the father. For many days he says no other words.

The brother looks at me with a blank face. I wait for him to kick my mouth.

My mouth he does not kick. He walks up to the father slumped in the chair. The brother puts his mouth up to the eye. A maggot crawls out of the eye and into brother's mouth. The brother swallows the maggot, looks me in the face and says mother. I repeat back to him mother. He picks a maggot from the eye and says open your mouth.

I walk up to the father, grab a handful, stuff my mouth full. I say mother again and again for the brother, my mouth stuffed full.

Z's Bones

When I was ten we broke into school me and Z. Z he was skinny so his body it fit in small spaces. The school was our school but this was not a day for students this was not a day for teachers. I lifted the trap door on the flat roof and watched the town for people the sun bright and hot. From the roof I could see the whole town I could see the ocean I could see cars and graves and boats and trees. There were so many graves in the graveyard it was close enough to see cracks in the graves dead flowers in the grass there were more graves than people in sight. There were no people the day was Sunday on Sunday the people of town all assembled in a big building with a bell this building just beyond the graveyard. The bell made sounds sometimes and it happened to be making the sounds it sometimes made when I opened the door as far as it could open and Z squeezed his body through. When Z took off all his clothes I could see most of his bones he still struggled to fit all I could do was watch. My bones were covered with fat I could not fit in small spaces. It was pitch black below the door latched with a rope and the rope tied loose to a ladder. Who tied the rope did not take into account a body like Z's. When Z got down there to where the ladder led he would untie the rope so I could pull the door open and I would climb down to join him we would be in the school. The bell on the building where the people assembled still made its sounds I listened because there were no other sounds to hear. When the rope slacked I lifted the door with ease light broke in I could see how far the ladder led down I could see Z. I listened for his voice in the space between the strikes of the bell I shut my eyes leaned close.

The Sister's Mouth

No one speaks. The sister sweats. She does not touch the plate. The sister out of breath. Stares at the face in the plate. She grips the fork in her hand. She shakes. The father smokes. Candles drip. The father flicks ash to the floor. With its tongue the dog laps it up. The skin of the brother burns. The father kicks the brother in the shin. The mother clears her throat, bares her teeth. The brother puts the plate in front of the sister. She knocks her knees on the table. The mother grabs the sister's wrist. Wipes the sister's face with a cloth. The sister drops the fork. It skips off the table to the floor. The dog barks. The father kicks it in the mouth. The brother puts the legs of the table back in place. The sister sits back. The mother points to the cake, carves lines in the air. In the light her face glows. She hums a low pitch. Tightens her grip on the sister. The sister keeps her eyes on the plate. She takes a breath. Blows out the flames. Back and forth she rocks. Her seat creaks. The record skips. The father stands. The brother pulls candles from the cake. Wax sticks to the icing and the brother's skin. The icing is mud. The mother keeps to herself. The brother holds his hand out below the table for the dog. The father drains the bottle. He clenches his teeth and chest, coughs, walks slow to the kitchen. The dog follows. With her fist the mother hits the table. The father stops. Turns the knob. He shifts it up and down but the sound stays the same. From the wall he rips the cord. The brother keeps his hands below the table. Holds one of the candles still wet from the dog. The sister does not blink. She touches her teeth, chews her lip. The father drifts to the kitchen's darkness. The dog's collar jangles. The mother cuts. Places cake on the plate. The sister's eyes light up. The father returns to the room, picks up from the floor the fork. Waves it in the sister's face, puts it back on the table. Mumbles to himself and sips from the bottle. The mother shoves the plate toward the sister. Rests the knife on the table. Wipes the fork with the cloth. Grabs the sister by the wrist and puts the fork in her hand. She wraps the sister's fingers one by one around the fork. The sister stabs the cake. Shovels it up to her mouth. Cake spills out from the sides of her lips. She licks what she can with her tongue. Licks the crumbs off the plate and table. Scrapes her face with the fork. Then she checks the space in her teeth for cake that is stuck. The plate wet with spit. A face like her face she sees in the plate. The face has no teeth. She taps her teeth with the fork. No holes or gaps. The face drips spit from its chin. The spit looks black. The sister licks it with her tongue. Rubs her skin with her hands, the insides of her mouth. Feels nothing on her face or in her mouth. She digs the fork at the plate. The mouth of the face opens. No sounds come out. The sister's mouth, she puts a fist in it. The mother shakes the knife in the air. The sister drops her hands to her sides. Feels the brother's hands on her skin. Hides her fists below the table. The brother is still. The father silent. The sister stares at the plate. The mother slices through the cake. She bares her teeth. Puts the cut piece on the plate.

The Spaces between Teeth

In the water of the lake we used to swim and float. Watch the sun watch us until our eyes blurred blind. Sometimes the sun got so hot there was no way to move. We watch them get lifted from the mud one by one by one. Rocks stuck to the skin of their faces not coming loose. We count twelve bodies before stopping to examine the boy. The boy's mouth is the one mouth they find does not close.

The only sound is the sound of the sun burning the lake. There is no telling how long the bodies have been here. They are wrapped tight in wire and cloth, facedown and stiff. They do not uncover the bodies before reaching into the mouths. They count missing teeth and then fill the buckets up. Brush clumps of dirt from the skin on the faces. Dirt clouds the air and rises up to the sun. The faces do not look like faces we have seen before now.

With hammers in hand they tap teeth in the mouths. The boy whose mouth does not close does not have teeth. We cannot see the movements of their hands in his mouth. They surround the boy's body all dressed in black or white. They become clouds of bodies themselves while working on the boy.

It has been twelve days since the bodies rose from the mud. The bodies float as if the mud were lake water. There is only the dark of night and the sun's heat. Cloth still covers the bodies and the men do not stop working. They are busy with the wires, busy with the faces. We move closer to see the details of the hands. They only stop to sleep at night, but do not sleep much. Only one stays awake to keep watch. He paces back and forth holding the hammer ready to hit. When birds fly on a face he swings the hammer just right.

They arrange the bodies in the mud at the top of the ditch. They grab the bodies by the ankles and lift them from the mud. It takes three of them to lift while one holds the hammer. The others wait at the bottom of the ditch. They make sure the skin does not scrape or peel or scratch. When a mistake is made they take a hammer to the mouth. They do not run or hide to avoid getting hit with the hammer. Into buckets they spit broken bits of teeth.

In wire and cloth we are wrapped and stuck facedown in mud. They spin us in circles and untangle the wire from the cloth. They hold hammers to our mouths and scrape the spaces between teeth. We are blinded by the sun and hear nothing but dirt. The dirt being dug next to our bodies, our heads, faces. They unwrap the cloth and our bodies ache and bulge and leak. Birds land on our faces and dig at our eyes, our mouths. We choke on their feathers when they get caught in our throats. Our throats dry and filled with dirt and heat and rocks. They brush the dirt-caked cloth and clouds fill the air.

After twelve years at the bottom of the lake we are seen. We cannot hear the hammer swing but feel it in our teeth.

The sun burns us awake. We did not know we slept. We hear breath from a mouth and the sinking suck of mud. As we step into the ditch our whole bodies ache. It has been twelve months since we have moved from the mud. Scattered about are feathers and bones, wires, cloth, skin. The bodies dry in the heat of the sun with eyes parched open. We watch them watch the sun, the sun watching them back. They dress in black or white or in nothing at all. When kicked in the face with boots they do not move. We try to speak but words clip and catch in our throats. We find a hole of dead birds and buckets filled with teeth. The parts of dirt not yet mud turn to mud.

We have no choice but to grab bodies for ourselves.

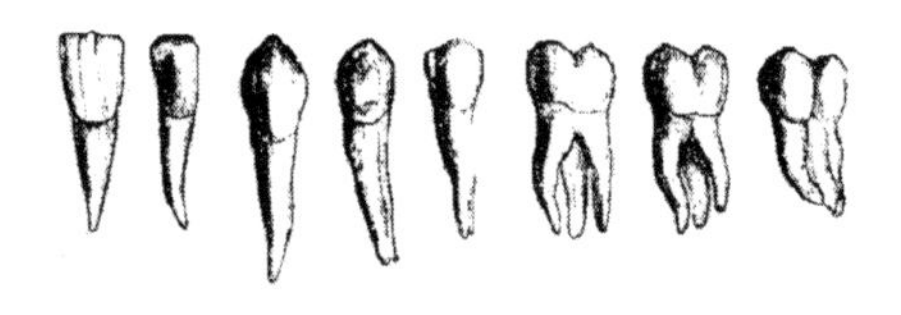

III.

ONE PINT
BOTTOMS UP

Drinking at the Dam

The mother is silent. Bowls lined with dirt line the deck. Broken glass on the floor. The doors, no locks. The father drinks. He leaves no note.

The sister says it happens at the lake.

The train tracks, she says.

In the backs of cars.

The road blurs.

He sits at the lake, waits. Sucks a bottle with his mouth. The sun beats his back.

The sister lights a match.

The song repeats.

The phrase loops.

The taste of the bar on her tongue, the smoke.

The father hits the mother. Hits her on the mouth.

Dogs bark. The sister's back digs in dirt. Rocks stick to skin, the backs of legs. On the deck the mother fills the bowls. The sister opens the car door.

The night is pitch black.

She opens her mouth.

No stars, no boat.

He dips her body under. Breathes into her neck. At the doorstep he leaves her.

She burns and bleeds while the mother sleeps.

She shuts the car door, the sister.

Staggers slow up the steps and leaves words as she walks: *I'm just drinking at the dam, I'm just drinking at the dam, I'm just drinking at the dam.*

This Noise Does Not Stop

(part one)

It was not long ago the boys used to creep through town night and day looking for god knows what. When they brought trouble back I gave them more to swallow.

Back then they used to fall to the floor crying, drooling, curled up. They would not amount to much, so I had no choice but to raise them rough.

I watched them get tossed from a truck.

I watched them fall from a top branch.

I watched them near-drown in a mud pool.

I kicked them in the ditch.

Touched their shaking bodies.

Ran my hands through their hair.
Said do you like the taste of dirt.
My own mouth I filled up.

They could not tell the difference between strays. Even lit one neighbor's cat aflame. They burned the back wall of the chicken coop. With animals they had no touch.

Dumb kid stuff some say, but with everything else unfolding I did not need much.

When they came home with arms broke or skin ripped open I said I told you so. I let them feel it. I said you are lucky he is not here anymore. Then I pointed.

I stayed looking at them. Watched their faces change.

He sat in a chair staring at stains on the wall. I cannot remember the days he was not fixed in a trance, looking off toward anywhere but here.

His eyes never locked with mine. Body fat and bloated, mind melted to mush. I used to get sad about it but I know I did my part. After awhile I let him be.

He turned pale as a clean sheet.

He even slept with eyes wide open. Looked touched by his own ghost. And a god-awful stench rose from his skin. I got used to it, but stopped letting the boys come up from the basement.

The day had seemed normal.

His appetite was still down and only getting worse as the days progressed so I shoved as much food into his mouth as I could fit. He turned whiter, but other than that nothing unusual was out of place. After we ate I lit the candles to cleanse the room. The room smelled the same. I opened the window and smoked. Stared at the same constellations. The sky was clear and bright. I drifted into a tranquil state, fought the weight of my lids. Dozed off till hot ash dropped on my thigh. I went to grab his hand out of habit but could not find it. Turned my whole body around to look. His chair was empty. No lines in the cushions, bumps or outlines that showed a trace of recent inhabitance. I thought he would at least leave a dent.

I do not remember much of what happened after. I know I checked in on the boys, then everything blurs. They were in their cage. Shivering a little, swaying back and forth, quiet as can be. I noticed the cage needed cleaning. Their limbs interlocked. Bodies pressed close. I did not want to disturb them, did not want to wreck their sleep to tell them their dad had disappeared.

I went back up to look, but my last vision is of the boys. The next, a blank.

When I awoke my head hurt. Ears filled with blood, everything out of place. Some of the lightbulbs did not work. Some had shattered. The fan in the kitchen unresponsive. The smoke detector with its piercing incessant pulse would not turn off until I ripped it from the wall, stomped it to bits. My notepad, where I keep lists and charts for the boys, turned from yellow to a pale blue. My handwriting was not my handwriting. The mop was not in the kitchen anymore. It was in the closet. My ears would not stop bleeding. They scabbed over quick, hardening in a matter of seconds before flowing down my neck in clumps.

I made a list of places to look:

_ roof
_ bedroom
_ bed
_ closet in bedroom
_ bathroom
_ cabinet below bathroom sink
_ kitchen
_ cabinet below kitchen sink
_ closet in hallway off kitchen
_ basement
_ below stairwell in basement
_ backyard
_ back shed
_ under wheelbarrow in back shed
_ truck
_ truck bed
_ doghouse
_ chicken coop
_ tree in backyard
_ tree in neighbor's frontyard
_ all trees in other neighbor's front- and backyards
_ both neighbor's houses
_ both neighbor's basements
_ both neighbor's bathrooms
_ both neighbor's trucks

- ditch at dead end of street
- river beyond ditch
- trees along river
- big rock on other side of river
- field on other side of big rock
- road on route to town
- bar in town
- bathroom in bar
- bartender's house in next town
- basement in bartender's house
- gas station beyond bartender's house
- gas station bathroom
- gas station back shed
- woods behind gas station
- graveyard beyond woods
- river beyond graveyard
- rocks along river
- bottom of river
- water in river
- back to ditch
- dead end

(part two)

Sometimes it is the noise from his mouth. Sometimes the noise comes from his throat. The noise low or the noise high. The low noise comes from his throat and the high noise from his mouth. Sometimes the noises switch. Or maybe it is the mouth and throat that do the switching. It is the sound of a noise stuck somewhere in between. The least favorite noise of all. Everyone agrees. Then everyone tells me do your job. Voices seep through the dirt. There is nothing else to say. I take nothing and go. The steps creak. The air reeks and I swallow too much. The noise increases. I cannot tell if it gets louder or picks up speed. Light a match to see. Pitch black. The match drops and burns out landing in dirt. It takes three matches to find the lantern. When I find the lantern I light it. Light fills the corner of the basement. I place the lantern on the stone where the wall goes in. All up and down the wall juts in and out. Solid yet about to collapse. Dust motes float slow motion through the lantern light. Dirt sifts through the cracks. I place my hands palm-up in the cage. His face and neck redden. He digs into dirt with his feet. More spit than usual dangles from his chin. It is thick as tar. The chain too tight. He cannot quite reach. He keeps trying. This is when I reach into the cage. He opens up a toothless mouth. His breath not hot or cold. I do not move my hand. He hacks and slips on leaks. The chain tightens. He climbs back to his feet. The chain jangles. I wait for him to come closer. He always does. I say the brother's name.

She starts on roof. Climbs ladder. On roof cannot see far. Roof is flat. Land flat. She sees trees, dirt, rock, river, neighbor houses, trucks, doghouse, chicken coop, back shed, ditch, dead end. She does not see anything beyond river, road, field, town, bar, gas station, houses on other streets, woods in other towns, graveyards, people. Nothing much on roof. Sticks, leaves, squirrel. Gun. She picks up stick. Pokes squirrel with it. Stiff. She covers squirrel with leaves. Lifts stick above shoulder. Aims stick at squirrel. She drives stick down through squirrel. Moves stick and squirrel to gutter. Covers squirrel with leaves. She leaves the stick sticking out. Picks up gun. Walks to edge of roof. Looks ahead at river. Tosses gun to dirt. Closes eyes. She breathes in. Eyes open. Breathes out. Jumps off roof.

Nothing in the bedroom. I looked in corners, closet, below bed, mattress, beneath sheets, pillows, even ran my hands along the ceiling to feel around. I cannot remember the last time we shared a bed. The room is eight by ten. I spent the night to make sure he was not there. Did not hear a thing but the boys in the basement. They sounded fine. Sooner or later I figured they would feel the lack. No boy deserves that. I waited for the sun before setting out. Every ounce of me said he was not in the house but I knew he was not far either. He could not be. I gave the kitchen a thorough search. Cabinets, sink, bathroom. Everything empty. When I went down to the basement the boys had gone silent sleeping. Could not even hear breathing. I checked the chains to make sure they were tight. Dragged them to a fresh spot in the dirt. Told them be good, I will be back soon. I glanced under the stairwell. Reached down to grab the lantern. I looked back at those boys.

Silence. I crawl against the cold wet wall to unfold. There are sharp points of stone, bits of gravel, moist dirt sticking to skin. Brother sleeps. Something scrapes against my throat. Stick a finger in but it is too deep. I hack out a black fluid that smacks on my stomach. I do not recall when the light began blinking. I do remember the back of an old woman walking up the steps. I am not leaning into the wall. I am on my back. The floor tight-packed with dirt and broken glass. Footsteps creak on floorboards sinking. Voices mutter to each other from which direction it is unclear. Dust and dirt spill down my face. I cannot shake the taste from my mouth.

In the backyard nothing but dead grass. In the back shed nothing but birds that are dead too. Beneath the wheelbarrow more dead birds. In the truck nothing but dead matches. Truck bed, nothing dead. In the doghouse piles of dog shit. In the chicken coop a dead dog. In the backyard tree nothing but dead leaves. Neighbor's frontyard a dead tree. Other neighbor's backyard a dead neighbor. Other neighbor's frontyard a dead neighbor's dead daughter. In the other neighbor's house nothing but dead space. In the dead neighbor's house it is dead quiet. In the other neighbor's basement dead rats. In the dead neighbor's basement deadbolts. The other neighbor's bathroom floods. In the dead neighbor's bathroom there is mud. In both neighbor's driveways dead trucks. In both trucks dead weight. On way to ditch nothing but dirt.

I jumped off the roof and landed on grass. Wiped the blood off my elbow and shook the impact from my bones. Grabbed the gun. Looked both ways down the dirt road. Nothing much for miles but I saw in the distance my destination through the leaves and branches and bark to the river carved by the shapes of the trees. I thought of things found in the past. Kept my eyes peeled and walked. The poor dead neighbor's dead daughter lay soaking in the heat. Dried up and distending. She did not budge when I gave a kick to the ribs. She never spoke much.

I got to the ditch and slid my body down. Picked up a rock. Threw it at the river. The rock ricocheted off a tree and did not hit water. It bounced off another rock, made a cracking sound then landed back on the ground. I walked toward it crunching through dead leaves and eyed the stillness of the river.

I wake to the sound of scraping. It does not take long for the scraping to stop. The silence does not last long either. Replaced by a low hum. It is hard to tell, I soon realize, if the hum has always been there, or if it was at first, to my ears, covered up by earlier sounds of scraping. The low hum could have always been there. The source of the hum unclear. I cannot tell if the hum comes from the dirt or somewhere in my bones. I can never quite catch hold. Try with all the strength in my hands to latch on but it avoids my grip. The source must be a body of its own.

If brother were here he would help.

If only the lights would turn on.

I forget about the hum and wonder how the scraping stopped.

As soon as I broke through the trees the sky opened up. Clouds swallowed by sun. I watched bodies float along the river. They moved slow but straight, nodded their heads on the way by. I stepped out into the clearing, felt jagged rocks through my boots. The heat hit my face. I could not get too close without sinking into mud. I eyed the big rock on the river's other side. The field behind glistened in the light. I set down in a dry patch. I could see just enough of the road on the other side to know no cars were on it. I walked along the river before slogging through. Maybe the boat was a sign. I thought of the boys. I thought would it not be nice to bring them home something good. I tiptoe down to the basement so as not to wake them. Rest my hand on their shoulders, give them each a gentle shake. Whisper in their ears what they have been waiting to hear. They start to say something and I say I know. I reach out a hand. One then the other. Drag them up the steps. Their bodies slide along old wood, legs stiff from sleep, and the moment when we bust through the basement door a beam of light comes through the window, settling on the chair. And he is there as if he never left.

Waiting for Water to Boil

In a cart they drag this body through the dirt along the rotting creek, the grass cutting up the sun-bleached surface of the mud, a trail of dead birds and gutted fish piled in puddles, covered in black oil and metal, bloating in the sun or ripped open to bone, wheels kicking rocks into the meat of calves, ankles, heels, feet, the sting shooting through tendon and bone, legs bent and hanging over the front lip of the frame, twitching and catching on dirt and rocks and dead blades of grass with the boys taking turns pushing the cart from behind, passing back and forth in their hands the cart's wood handles, the hammer and the blade, both boys with hollow, black eyes and busted teeth, thick scars on their chins, pushing and dragging this body up and down the ditch and back up the hill past this broken fence to the red barn in the dirt, the barn's sounds singing from the baler and the shredder and the pulley and the rope, the hammer hitting the steel latch of the gate, the clippers cutting the wire in two and these boys they shove a wet rag in its mouth and the back of this tongue and throat hack at the crumpled-up rag and the boys keep swinging again and again at its mouth with the back of the hammer, spit clenching to this throat, no wool or cloth to shield this skin from the sun, no soaking up of this blood, the smell of oil and rust, the scraped-out rot of a stomach, the burned-off hair from a groin and chest, bite marks scattered from the teeth of a dog, but these boys, with their scars on their chins and their busted teeth, these boys they dance in this mud with blood around their mouths, like hogs hanging from hooks, waiting for water to boil, waiting for this skin to be scraped clean and cut.

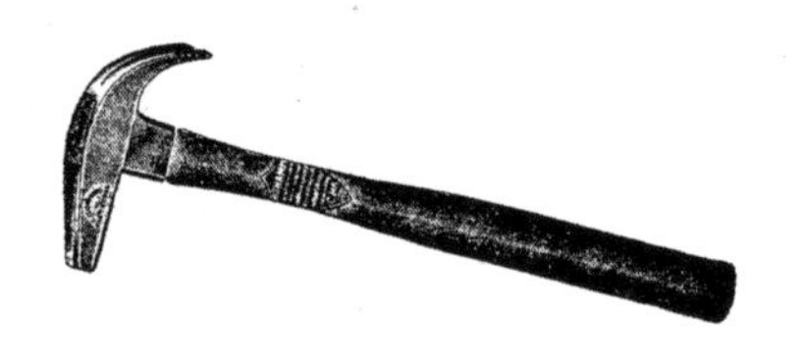

Let Me See the Colts

I must not blink with hammer in hand.

Sometimes when I blink I miss the nail and hit bone. Once I split my thumbnail into little pieces, lost in the gravel.

I drive the spikes deep into soil.

Bolt an anchor to each corner of the frame.

When the floor-frame fits I set the wood on top. I must not bounce on the floor when I walk.

I reach for a nail in the bucket.

Grind my teeth to scrape.

When there are no more nails in the bucket I walk to town. The center of the town is where they keep the nails.

They expect meat in exchange but I have no meat with me now.

Before I walk to town I must find the

nails in the soil or gravel or back of the barn.

When I wash the bodies at night I check for lumps that sometimes grow inside the stomach. If lumps get inside the stomach there is no way to tell till the day I find the body collapsed on the floor of the stall.

In the bucket I must keep track of the nails.

I must hammer the nails sticking out of the wood that catch on skin.

When bodies collapse in the stalls they are hard to pull out in one piece.

I flip my boots upside down so the bottoms face the sky. The tops of the boots sit flush with the soil. If they do not sit flush there will be enough space for a snake or rodent. There are more rodents in these woods and the grass and the barn than I know how to name. When I find them in boots there is no way to tell just by bones or teeth. I scoop them out and wash my feet in the creek. When a rodent or snake gets stuck in a bale they shoot out through the shredder. When they shoot through the shredder the meat and bones and teeth mix with the feed. I try to keep critters away but there is no way to know if they are chewed up and spit out till

I open the door to a body on its back. I know colic when I see it. No matter what I must check the color of the mucus in the mouth. Touch inside to feel my way around. If I move too quick the skin will tear. I must slow down. Slide my arm in slow. I have seen them kick through a stomach. The nose twitch clamps to the upper lip with a chain, ring, rope. I must wait for the skin wrapped tight around my arm to relax. For the skin to let go. I wait for it to empty itself out.

●

I strap the feedbag to my back.

The hammer hangs in its holster on the belt. I lock the gate latch, the slide bolt on the fence. The meat sits in a bucket on a brick of dry ice.

The dirt road runs into the center of town. I must return to the barn before dark.

If they refuse the meat I will slide the hammer from the holster.

I pull the picture from my pocket.

Black wires coil around the belly and throat.

A loose stack of bricks leans against a broken sink.

White foam forms at the mouth.

Shattered bottles soak in puddles of curdled milk.

Stained yellow ribbons hang from pipes.

A body stiff on its back, a bag of sand.

I trip on a metal sign half hidden in dirt. I read the words the sign says but no sound comes out.

I kiss it on the mouth.

The boys keep their mouths shut. The one with the limp drops a strap. I hang to one side above a broken bottle, a puddle of oil. He dusts off the chair in front of the window. Sets bricks in place of the missing legs. Bites the wire between his teeth, tears at the cloth. I put my hand to my cheek and feel bone. The sting of it shoots through my skull, down to my toes. They stuff my mouth with a handful of cushion. The boy with the chain holds up scissors. On his hands, instead of thumbs, are little black stumps. The boy with the limp scrapes the blade, cuts the cloth, sets it on the sill. The steel chain drags on wood. They lift me by the straps. Wires cut into the skin of my back. I spit the cushion back out. They hit me in the teeth with the hammer, push my face to my lap. They rip wires from the chair, dump nails from the bucket. The wire wraps around my mouth and down my back, thighs, ankles, feet. A piece of loose skin gets pulled from my wrist. Palms up, thumbs out straight, the nail drives through skin in one strike. The blood dries in thick lines before it puddles. They wet the claw of the hammer with their mouths. The boy with the limp looks me in the eyes, bares busted teeth. The other boy puts his fist in my mouth. The black stump tastes of milk and spit. They drag their tongues up and down my stomach and chest. Suck the cuts on my ribcage clean. I see my face in the glass, cracked and boarded up with wood painted black. On the sill the scraper sits. Skin hangs from the bone of my cheek. The hands with the stumps lift the bag to my face. They dump feed in my lap. The feet on the bodies are cut. The bellies bloated and burned, the eyes do not shut. The boy with the stumps cups a body in his palms. The other boy opens the scissors, rests them on the neck, snips. I hear the twitch of my eyes in their sockets. When I swallow, the skin on my throat gets cut.

When the skin tears, it sticks to wood.

Skin sticks to broken glass and puddles.

Skin sticks to the bucket in my hands, my own face and mouth.

The dogs leave nothing in the stomach. No bones for them to suck. They lick the eyes and nose, mouth and throat. They each take a leg in their mouth, tug until it splits. The legs hang loose from their teeth, drip in the dirt. The one walks with a limp, the other drags a chain from its foot. The front door cracks open, the dogs slip inside. All I see behind the door is blackness before it shuts. When the latch locks, I walk to where the body is. No bones, no skin, no meat. All I find is an old blade, a razor, studded with rust. I slide the blade in my mouth between my tongue and teeth. The chain hits the wood behind the door of the house. Boards on the windows shake. The sound stuck in a throat. There are no nails in the bucket. No hammer hangs from my holster. No meat on a brick of dry ice. I fill the bucket to the top with rocks. Reach between my teeth and tongue and pull out bone.

I watch the birds twitch in the dirt. The pipe tied tight to my pocket. If the sound does not stop I drop them in the bucket, tear a piece off the cloth. Stuff it in their mouths, then kick them in the ditch. Like this the bucket fills up. If the birds still twitch I carve a name upon their stomachs. I lie down in the dirt, cup the holes in my chest. Tear a nail half off with teeth. Grip the claws, line the pipe up to the eyes. The meat of my tongue hangs loose from this mouth. The birds flap. I cut my own stomach up. Fill both fists with this mud. The birds land claw-first on my hair, forehead, eyebrows, nose, cheekbones, lips, tongue, chin, neck, chest.

The birds fill their mouths with mud.

They scoop eye-meat from the sockets.

Grind up tissue in the tongue.

Uncoil rings below the eyes.

I choke on nail, cloth, bone.

Choke on claw, teeth, mud, milk, spit, fat, meat.

Maggots crawl from the wood.

The lumps inside the stomach split.

The stomach, what burns inside it, kicks.

The man points to tools hanging from hooks. Blisters cover his knuckles. He scratches a rash on his wrist. The rake I slide from the hook. With the back of the hammer he digs. Takes a step closer, makes a slow sucking with his mouth. Light shines through glass. I see nothing through the skin on his face. His knuckles white with puss. I toss the rake to the dirt.

He speaks this from the gut.

The stalls in the barn, he says.

The walls, grills, gates.

Wood, nails, he says.

Bone.

From his neck the cloth hangs.

He wipes his mouth. The hair on his skin in patches. The rash cracks around the base of the throat. I look back at the hooks.

He says the tarp is laid out flat.

He says chains, straps, twine, bucket, rope, tractor, hoe.

Shovel, he says.

The sun glints off the steel of blade.

In a day, maybe two, the muscles will relax.

A tight fit, he says.

With the hammer he scoops puss from his knuckle. Spits.

Says open your mouth.

When I open my mouth he rips a nail from the wood.

This is what happens, he says, when you unlock the latch.

He lifts the blade from the hook, touches his tongue to the rust. Hands me the handle, the nail. Drops the hammer to the dirt.

His fist--he shoves his whole fist in my mouth.

Time to scrape, he says.

He steps away from the blade. The rust tastes muddy. The rag he rings out in the bucket.

The boys take turns. Back and forth in their hands they pass the cart's wood handles, the hammer and blade. Birds line the path along the creek. No cloth covers my skin. When the birds' bodies twitch, one of the boys lifts the hammer. The handle of the hammer is wrapped with ribbon, the steel covered in rust and dried-on mud. The boy's hand has no thumb, just a black stump where a thumb should be.

With the bodies of birds the cart fills up. The claws and bones dig at my neck, throat, ribs, stomach.

Both boys have hollow black eyes, busted

teeth, thick scars on their chins. One walks with a limp, the other drags a chain from his foot. My eyelids seal shut against the heat.

They push and drag the cart in the dirt up and down the ditch and back up the hill and past the broken fence to the red barn. Sounds in the barn sing from the baler and the shredder, the pulley and rope. The wire loosens from my mouth, the chain hits wood. With a rusted nail they peel my eyes back open.

Limbs laid out flat on the tarp.

Pitch fork, rake, shovel, sickle, scythe, grinder, clippers, cutters, pipe.

The men turn their backs, straps hang loose from their belts.

Light floods the stalls.

My eyes stick to the tarp.

The door again slams shut.

The one with the limp climbs the ladder. No bales or bundles between the floor and peak, no straw or hay to tie with twine.

The shredder sits at the base of the baler, its circling teeth.

The one with the black stumps shoves a wet rag in my mouth. The rag tastes of curdled milk. The boy drags the chain to the tarp.

The birds in the cart twitch.

Light creeps in through cracks in the barn.

I keep eyes locked on the tarp, spit the rag in the dirt.

The one in the loft says--*let me see the colts.*

Before this boy with the black stumps reaches for the tarp, the birds in the cart rise up to the top of the barn. They swarm and sing--these birds--mouths full of meat. I drop to the dirt, crawl to the tarp. The red barn shakes. The boy reaches down and fills both fists with muscle and fat. From the hook I lift the shovel. Dig a ditch next to the tarp. From the dirt I pull wire, cloth, bone, boots. In the ditch I lay down, open my teeth for the meat. I hear the pulley and rope, the sound of rocks shooting through the chute. Dirt hits my face, neck, chest, gut, groin, legs, feet. The birds' song cuts right through it.